P9-DCF-847

MEGAN'S BOOK OF DIVORCE

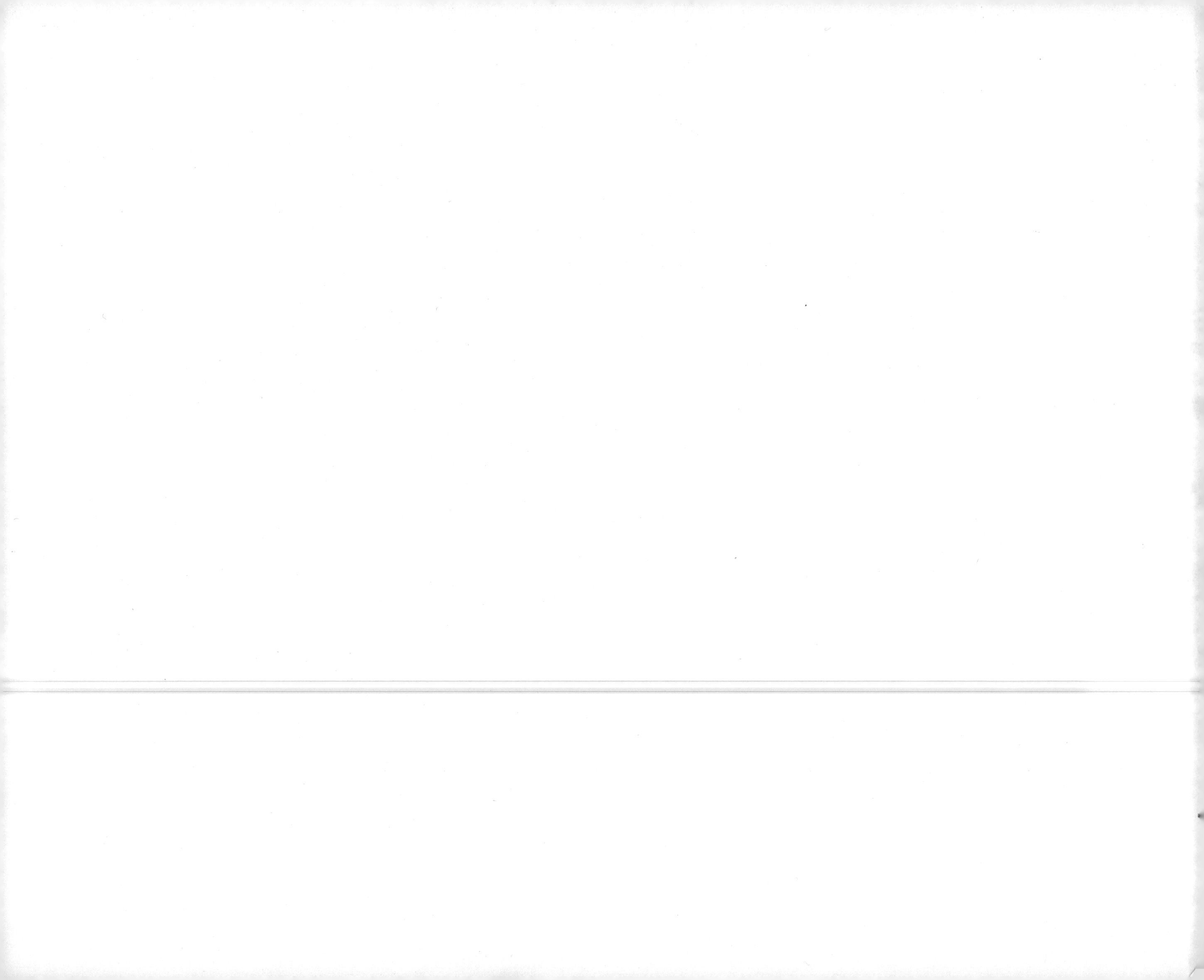

MEGAN'S BOOK OF DIVORCE

A KID'S BOOK FOR ADULTS

AS TOLD TO

ERICA JONG

Illustrated by Freya Tanz

NAL BOOKS
NEW AMERICAN LIBRARY
NEW YORK AND SCARBOROUGH, ONTARIO

Published simultaneously in Canada by The New American Library of Canada Limited

NAL BOOKS TRADEMARK REG. U.S. PAT. OFF. AND FOREIGN COUNTRIES
REGISTERED TRADEMARK—MARCA REGISTRADA
HECHO EN HARRISONBURG, VA., U.S.A.

SIGNET, SIGNET CLASSIC, MENTOR, PLUME, MERIDIAN and NAL BOOKS
are published *in the United States* by New American Library,
1633 Broadway, New York, New York 10019,
in Canada by The New American Library of Canada Limited,
81 Mack Avenue, Scarborough, Ontario M1L 1M8

Library of Congress Cataloging in Publication Data
Jong, Erica.
Megan's book of divorce as told to Erica Jong.

Summary: Irrepressible, four-year-old Megan gives
her own views on divorce.
[1. Divorce—Fiction] I. Tanz, Freya, ill. II. Title.
PS3560.056M6 1984 813'.54 83-24665
ISBN 0-453-00459-8

Designed by Julian Hamer and Freya Tanz

First Printing, May, 1984

1 2 3 4 5 6 7 8 9

PRINTED IN THE UNITED STATES OF AMERICA

For all kids who
have two houses
and for all the adults
they take care of

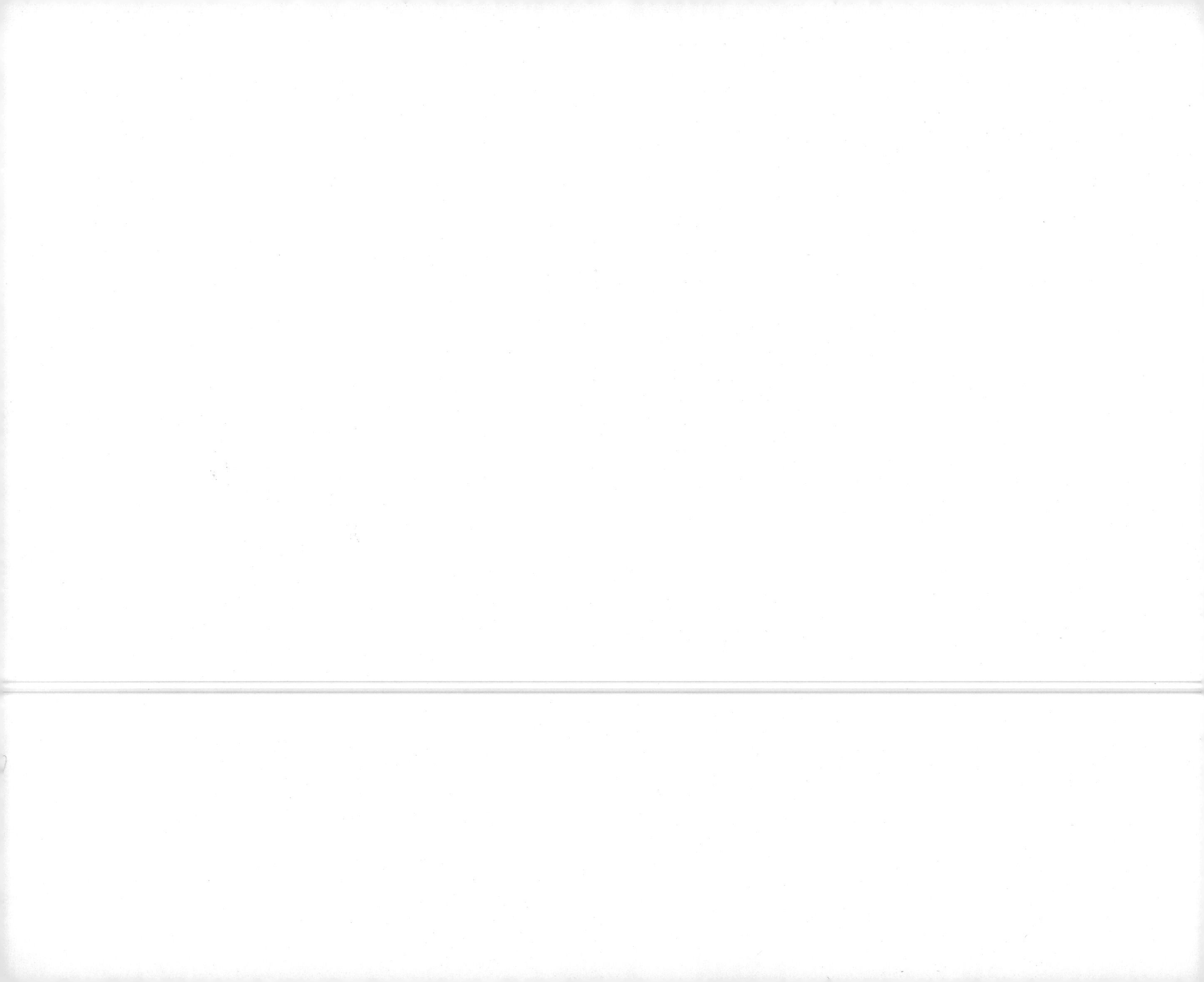

I am Megan.
I am four, but everyone says I am six.

Here's why:
I am tall and know words like "diagonal"
and "croissant."

I live in California.
My parents are separated.
That means they still like each other,
but they can't live together.

They don't *act* like they like each other.
Because they fight.
They are getting divorced. They both have lawyers.
They both have headaches.
They are arguing over copper pots and
who gets the piano.
I have to put up with them.
Adults are so incompetent.

FRAGILE
HANDLE WITH CARE

I think divorce is dumb
because I never remember
where I left my underpants.

I have two dogs,

two kitchens,

COOK

two toy chests.

Sometimes I want my ice-cream barrettes
and they're at Daddy's.
Sometimes I want them, and they're
at Mommy's.

But usually, one barrette is at Mommy's
and the other at Daddy's.
That's the other reason
divorce is dumb.

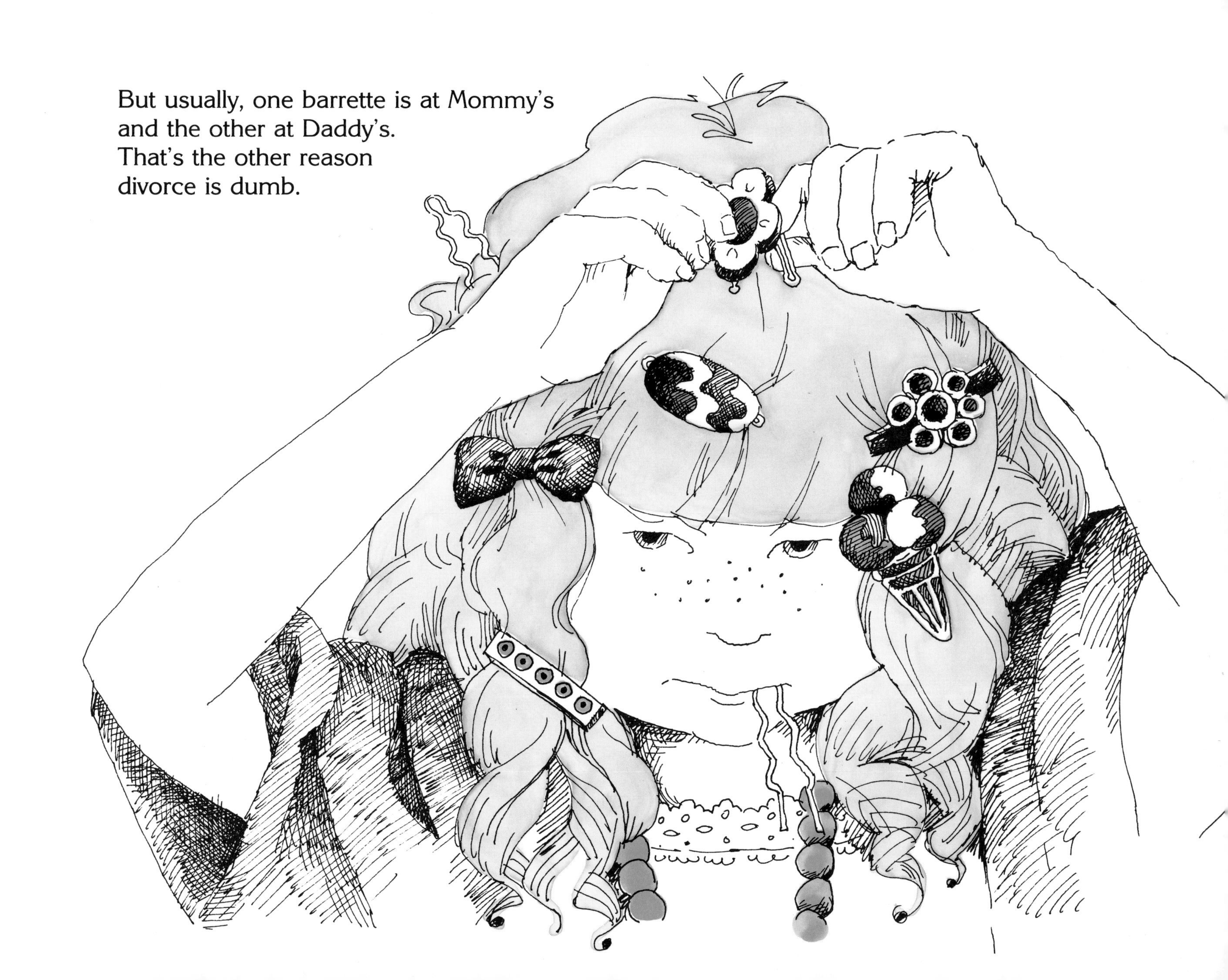

Divorce is also dumb
because you have to put up with your
parents' other friends.

My parents are both screenwriters.
When they lived together back East, my Dad wrote
in the garage and my Mom wrote in the attic.
I was just a baby. I slept in a carriage
on the porch and one of my nannies rocked me.

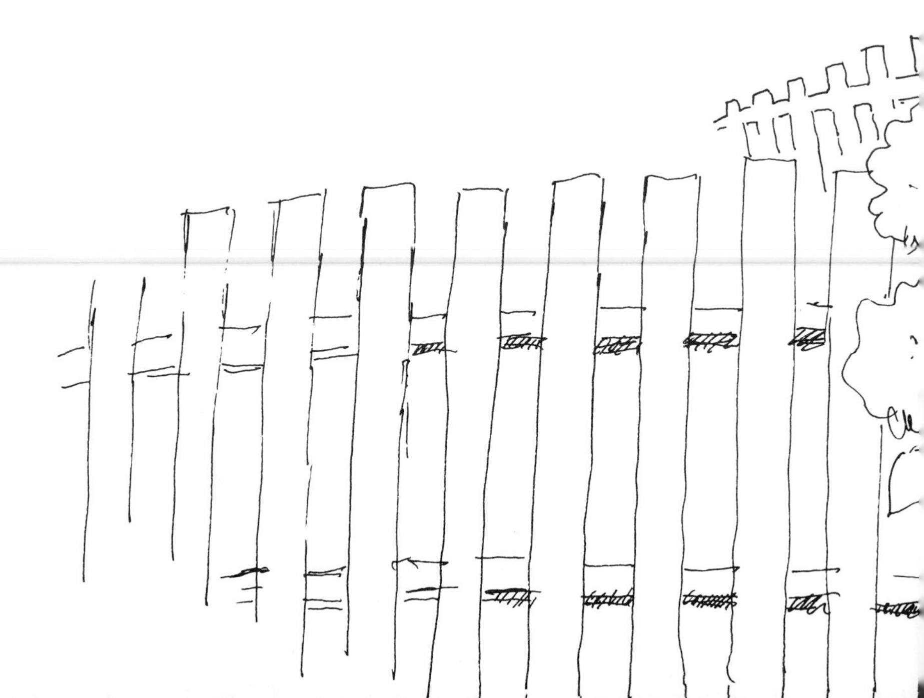

Here are the nannies I had:
Bessie-Lou who had healin' hands and took me to meet her pastor in Harlem. Hallelujah!

Annie-the-English-nanny-from-Blackbourne
who ran off with the roofer.

Moira-the-Moonie
and the less-said-
of-her-the-better.

Mona-from-Arizona
who ran off with the vegetarian.

Karin-from-Copenhagen who ran off with the yoga teacher who was a girl.

And now I have Mrs. Valley. Mom calls her Nurse Valium because she's so slow. I am fast. I love Nurse Valium. She lets me do anything when my Mom's not around. Especially watch grown-up TV and eat chocolate.

Now my Dad has a friend
and my Mom has a friend.
My Dad's friend is a
police detective.
Her name is Kate.
She puts bad guys in jail.
I like that.
I would like her to
put Mom's friend in jail.

When we speed
on the freeway,
she flashes
her badge and
we just keep speeding.
I like that.

5739-AP

But I do not like the way she fusses over me as if she wanted to be my Mommy. She will never be my Mommy. Here's what I do when Kate fusses over me. I say, "Kate, don't be so hectic." Sometimes she cries. Sometimes she brings me presents whether I deserve them or not.

My Mom's friend is an actor, but a lot of the time he is resting. Actors rest a lot. His name is Win. He has this dumb name because his real name is four last names: Winthrop Wilson Whittaker Waring, IV. He is "Win," but I usually call him "Lose." He hates this.

Sometimes it makes him cry.
He brings me flowers
whether I deserve them or not.

My Mom says: "Megan, you may hate anyone
you please in *private*, but you may not
hurt people's feelings."

I say: "Can I say I hate him when he's not in the room?"
Mom looks confused. She looks that
way a lot. Here's what I do to Win:
Kick him and say, "I hate you."

Here's why: If he gets mad and goes away, my Mom and Dad will have to put up with each other again and I can have all my barrettes and underpants in one house.

Here are my two dogs.
At my Mom's house, my dog is Emily Doggenson.
She's a Bichon Frise. She's a Champion, which
means she goes to dog shows and sends home ribbons
and bills. Mom says it's like having a kid in college.
Win calls her a Megastar, which is what he'd like to be.

Here's what I do with Emily Doggenson: teach her
French. "Chien" is "dog" in French. Emily cannot say
it. She cannot say "dog" in American either.
Here are the languages I speak: American,
French, and Spanish. "House" in Spanish
is "casa." "Water" is "agua." Our housekeeper,
Rosa, told me. She is Chicana
and lives in the barrio.

MEGA

At my Dad's house my dog is Scruffoon.
Here's why: She's from the pound and when we got her she was all scruffy. "Foon" is from "telefoon" which is "telephone" in Dutch. Once, when my parents were happy, they went to Amsterdam and bought an old brass "telefoon" which my Mom still has in her bathroom.

She sometimes talks on it from her bubblebath. After they got that "telefoon" my Mom and Dad called everything "foon"—even the dog.

I'm lucky they didn't call me Megoon. But almost. They called me Megan Melissa, which is enough.

When I want to get my Mom upset, I tell her I am changing my name to "Buster."

NOW

Scruffoon is a Polish Terrier, which is really a mutt. She looks just like the dog in *Annie*. Nobody knows how old she is. Not even the pound people. She was lost and my Mom picked her up and saved her. I think that's how my Mom found Win, too.

My Mom takes in strays. She's big-hearted but dumb. Win calls himself "The Vagabond." He calls Mom "Bounce," because she walks like a bouncing ball. I walk that way, too. I am the only kid in California with so much bounce.

Here's how I am going to get Mom and Dad together again: make Win cry a lot until he leaves. And make Kate cry so she can't put bad guys in jail.

I tell Kate: "Daddy
will never marry you,
so just give up."

I tell Win:
"Mommy will marry
you if you don't
watch out."

I tell Kate: I like Louisa better and so does Daddy."
I tell Win: "I like Doug better and so does Mommy."
Louisa is Daddy's other friend and Doug I just made up. Mommy's other friend is really Fred. I like him because he never hugs Mommy except when he thinks I'm asleep. Win hugs Mommy all the time.

I tell him: "Don't hug Mommy."
He says: "Somebody has to hug your Mommy."
I say: "I will do it! Or let Doug."

He says to Mommy: "Who the heck is Doug?"

Louisa is Jeremy's mother. Jeremy is five
and I am going to marry him.
Then we can have a baby
and get divorced.

Louisa and Daddy used to close the door to the bedroom so Jeremy and I could play divorce. Then one day Louisa cried a lot and yelled at Daddy almost as if they were married. I said:
"Are you playing divorce, too?"
But Louisa just cried.
Grown-ups cry
even more than kids.

For a while I didn't see Jeremy at all. But then Louisa and Jeremy came back. Louisa had another boy with her named Sidney. He was a lawyer who got bad guys *out* of jail.
I am not going to let him meet Win.

I am a kid so I have lots of time to think things up while everyone else is writing.

Mom writes in Malibu
with Emily Doggenson
under her desk.

Dad writes in Santa Monica
with Scruffoon
under his desk.

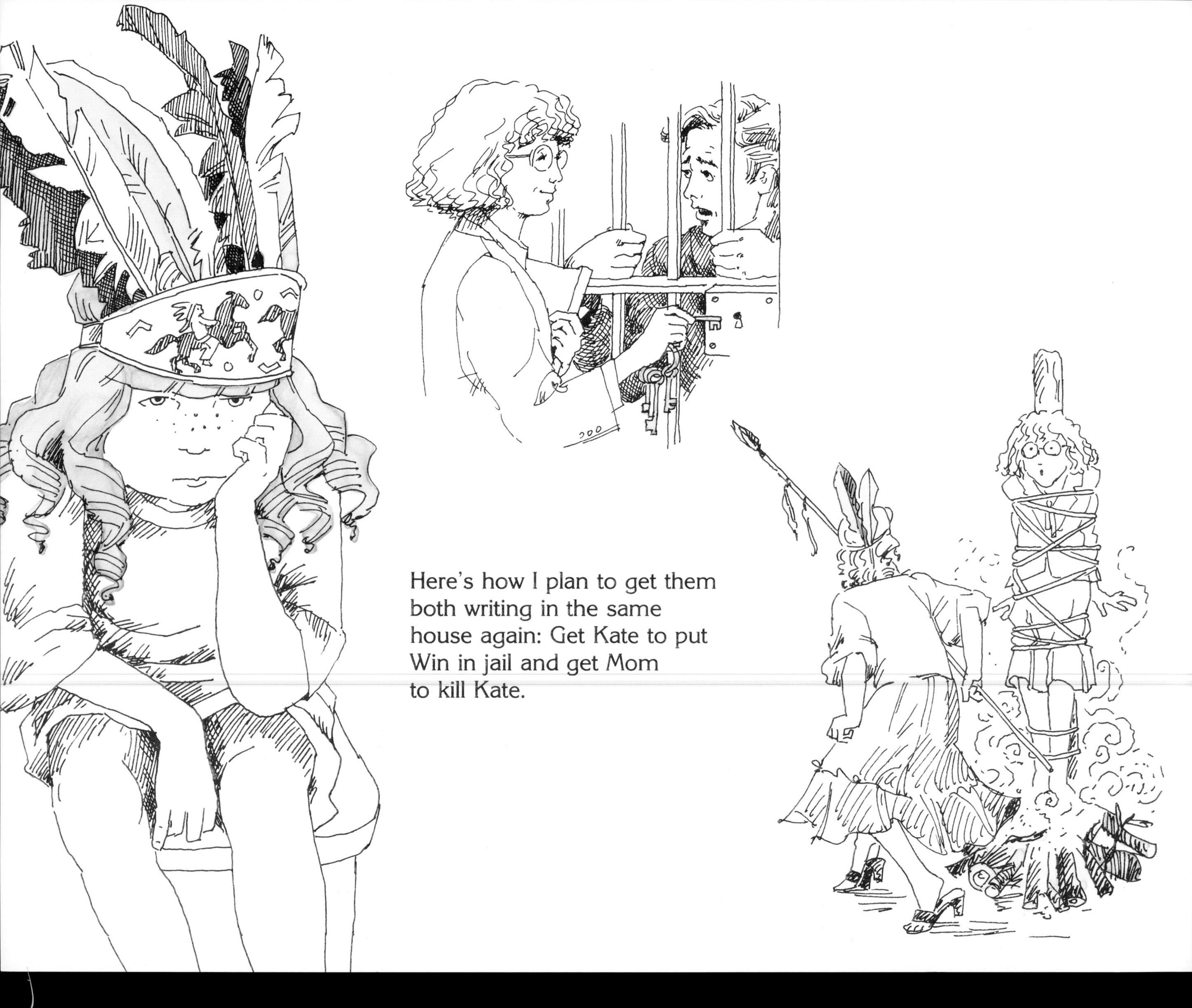

Here's how I plan to get them
both writing in the same
house again: Get Kate to put
Win in jail and get Mom
to kill Kate.

Get Dad to hug Mom when Win goes to jail.
Get Mom to hug Dad when Kate dies.

“What’s up, tootsie?” Daddy asks when I am thinking this stuff. I say: “I’m not going to tell you.”

“What’s up, lover?” Mom asks when I am thinking this stuff. I say: “I’m not going to tell you.”

But here's the amazing thing: they *know*.

"Divorce is not your fault," Mom says. "You didn't do anything wrong."

"Divorce *is* dumb," says Daddy, "but you can't do anything about it even if you try."

Here's why they're wrong: I, Buster, have a plan.

Next weekend, which is a Mommy weekend, I will sneak into Mommy's room while she and Win are sleeping in the brass bed and lasso Win's foot.

He taught me this.
I told you he was dumb.

Then I will press the button
on Mom's total phone that
get's Daddy's house.
Daddy's number is: 4.
Daddy will answer. "There's a bad
guy in Mommy's bed," I will say.
"Come over right away. Help! Help!"

And they will come.

And bring extra policemen, and Kate will lock Win in jail and throw away the key.

And Mommy will kill Kate.
And Daddy will cry.
And Mommy will hug Daddy. And I will hug them both. And we'll all say: "Divorce is dumb."
And we'll live happily ever after, like in Cinderella.

But here's what *really* happened.

Last Sunday was a Mommy Sunday. And when Win and Mommy got up, Kate and Daddy and Scruffoon came to brunch. And Daddy made special pancakes and Win made special poached eggs. And Kate made coffee. And Mommy made Bloody Marys, whatever they are. And I drank a Virgin Mary, which is a sort of tomato juice but yucky.

And we all sat down at the big round dining room table.

And Scruffoon and Emily Doggenson begged at table.
And Daddy said: "Oh, you ill-mannered dogs."
And Mommy laughed and didn't fight with Daddy.
And Mommy said, "Cheers!" and "Here's to old friends."
And I said: "Cheers."
Everyone hugged everyone, especially me.

And I fed Emily pancakes under the table.

And I fed Scruffoon eggs under the table.

And I said: “Divorce is dumb.”
But really I was thinking divorce wasn’t so bad if the fighting stopped and everyone got pancakes.

And anyway, I knew that nothing was my fault.

Not even Emily’s manners.
Not even Scruffoon’s manners.
Not even Win hugging Mommy.
Not even Kate being hectic.
Not even Dad fighting with Jeremy’s Mom.
Not even Jeremy saying he is going to marry and divorce another girl, not me.

Not even having two houses and never knowing where your underpants and barrettes are.

Not even missing Dad at Mom’s house and Mom at Dad’s house.

Because if they all stop fighting, you can have four grown-ups to hug you instead of two and twice as many presents every birthday.

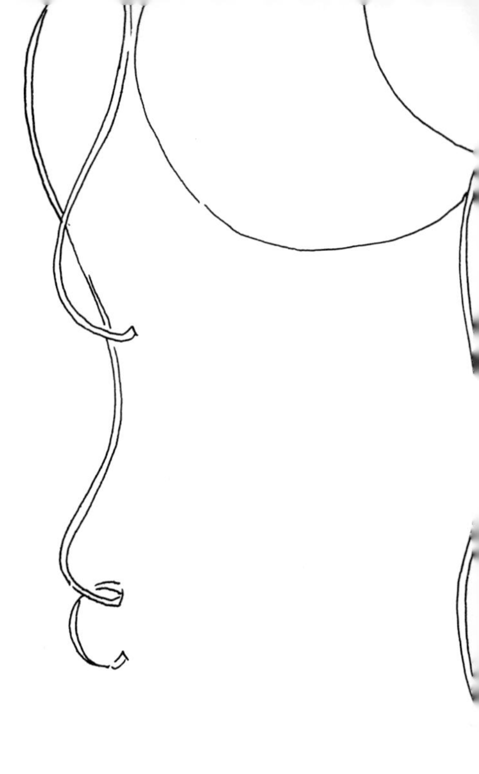

But I think I may still change my name
to Buster, after all.